DATE DUE

MY 27 '93		
JUN 27 '94		
JUL 28 '95		
FEB 27 '97		
JL 29 '30		
HR 25 '02		
AG 26 '7		

OINK OINK

Arthur Geisert

Houghton Mifflin Company

Boston 1993

For Noah

Library of Congress Cataloging-in-Publication Data

Geisert, Arthur.
  Oink, oink / Arthur Geisert.
    p. cm.
    Summary: Eight piglets wander off while their mother is still
sleeping and enjoy a feast in a cornfield before she brings them
home again. Story told with one word.
    ISBN 0-395-64048-2
    [1. Pigs—Fiction.   2. Mother and child—Fiction.]   I. Title.
PZ7.G27240j 1993   92-31778
[E]—dc20   CIP
                      AC

Printed in the United States of America

HOR 10 9 8 7 6 5 4 3 2 1

OINK OINK

OINK

EAU CLAIRE

OOOOOOOINK

OINK OINK OINK OINK OINK OINK OINK OINK OINK OINK OINK OINK OINK OINK OINK OINK OINK

OOOOINK

OOOOOOOINK

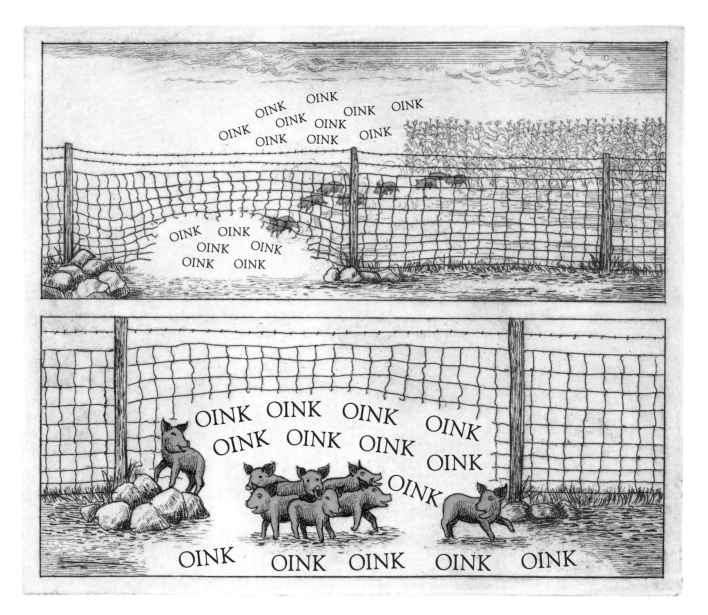

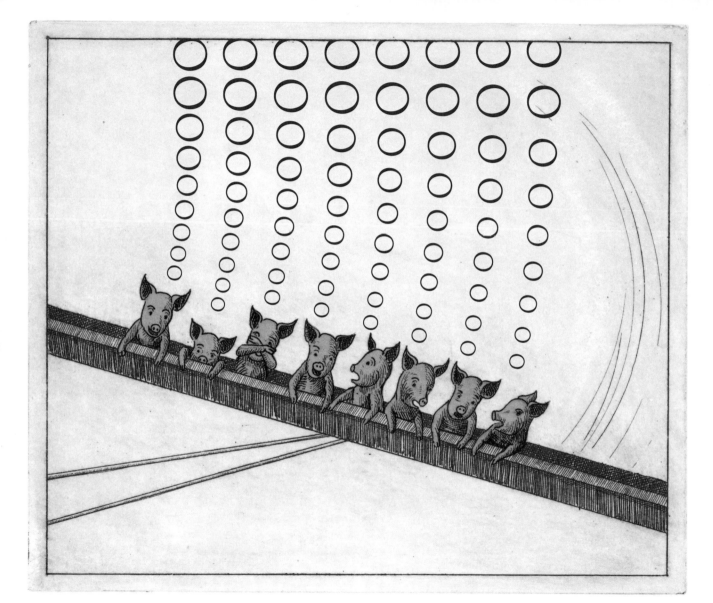

OINK OINK